The

COMEBACKER

McSWEENEY'S
SAN FRANCISCO

The

COMEBACKER

by

DAVE EGGERS

McSWEENEY'S

For Lindsay, Jon, Rob, Tony and Markus

THE DAY WAS COLD, cold even for August in San Francisco. As Lionel walked over the Lefty O'Doul Bridge, the wind seemed to be coming from every direction—the Pacific, the Bay, the brackish creek underfoot. And with every step, Lionel's left shoe squeaked, an especially maddening thing, given he'd just had them resoled. For years he'd passed a subterranean shoemaker's shop, thinking it would be old-timey and fun to ask the ancient Romanian proprietor to repair his shoes. Finally Lionel entered the man's tiny shop, crowded with bent boots and single loafers, and asked to have his favorite leather shoes, so soft they felt like moccasins, resoled. It felt very good, the whole encounter, until Lionel retrieved the shoes a week later and found the left one now let out a cartoonish squeak with every footfall.

When Lionel went back to the shoemaker, the old man shrugged. "Some shoes squeak," he said.

"But it's a new sole," Lionel said. "*You* put it on."

"*You* picked it out," the shoemaker said, and he was right. Lionel had flipped through a catalog of soles and had chosen the new one.

"Listen," Lionel said, and walked around the shop, squeaking.

The old man watched, listened, but wasn't the least concerned. "Some soles squeak," he said.

Lionel had learned to walk on the edge of his left foot. This diminished the sound, but gave him a worrying gait. People at the stadium had begun asking him about it. "It's nothing," he'd say. "It's just this left one, when I got them resoled, so…" He couldn't find the words.

Lionel covered the Giants for the *Examiner*, the home games at least. The paper, one of the city's two remaining dailies, didn't have the budget to send him on the road. There wasn't much to write, anyway. The season was effectively over; the team had no chance at the playoffs. The crowds were sparse, and the players had little to say. Not that they were so garrulous in winning, either.

They had mastered the art of fulfilling their obligation to stand at their lockers before and after games, answering questions while saying nothing. Lionel had been on the Giants beat for six years, but the job had reached its nadir with Marion Coletti. After some trouble with a certain left fielder, the team had brought in Marion to head the media relations department, and she'd drilled the players on verbal discipline. They learned how to string a few dozen words and phrases together, day after day, word clusters that made sense but meant nothing. "Trying to contribute." "Just focused on getting the win." "Great team effort." "Happy to be here."

The players were never unfriendly. That was bad PR, too. Marion taught them to be cheerful, accommodating, and dull. And Lionel duly printed their inanities. "Nice work, Lionel," Marion said when she approved of something he'd written. It was a terrible thing, to be praised this way.

Marion was from Montreal, and strode around the stadium in beautiful suits, sunglasses above her forehead, embedded in her raven hair. The effect, for the reporters at least, was a feeling that they were being doubly watched by this sophisticated, bilingual Canadian. As if aware of her imperious affect, she often brought in treats—candy, cupcakes, huge bars of artisanal chocolate from her native land. She was polished and warm, but had no qualms about limiting access if a reporter crossed her.

"Two-way street," she liked to say. So Lionel had traded candor for access, and loathed himself for it. He hadn't written anything memorable in months.

He and every other reporter were complicit. More than that—they'd created the problem. The reporters were in their forties and fifties and sixties, standing at the lockers of players half their age or less, hoping to get sticky quotes. "Get me sticky," Lionel's editor, Warren Spiwak, demanded.

The problem was that when a player said something even vaguely sticky—*sticky* was Warren's word for memorable, colorful, controversial—the sportswriters pounced, and often the player paid the price.

Apologies followed, and disappointed fans, and some-times lost endorsement deals, then, worst-case, a trade and a new team. That, or a player could just keep his mouth shut.

Squeak, squeak, squeak.

The sound was louder the closer he got to walls, to any structure; impossibly, it echoed. Lionel arrived at the stadium's media gate and showed his pass.

"Hi Shawna," he said.

Shawna was in her seventies, had worked for the Giants since the eighties. She had a pageboy haircut and a smoker's wheezy voice.

"Lionel," she said. "Still squeaking, I see. Or hear."

She scanned his barcode.

"Thank you. That's a wonderful observation, Shawna," Lionel said. "You're wonderful."

"Heard you coming the second you left your apart-ment!" she yelled as he stepped into the stadium.

Squeak, squeak, squeak. He knew it would get louder inside, where the narrow pathways in the bow-els of the building amplified every cough and thump. He thought seriously about going home and changing into sandals.

Lionel lived in a small isosceles triangle three blocks from the park. The neighborhood was changing, new condos rising daily, but his place was a leftover from the pre-stadium days. His building was still light-industrial—about fifty tenants ranging from T-shirt shops to film archivists to food photographers. The building wasn't zoned for residential use, so Lionel wasn't supposed to be living there, but the tenants felt their businesses were safer in the small hours with someone sleeping there, so everyone looked the other way. He paid a thousand a month, and shared a bathroom with a bearded couple—both of them so tall—who shot low-budget green screen commercials for local car dealerships.

Lionel made his way through the dim hallways, passing a dozen Giants ushers, staffers, and trainers, and showed his lanyard to Jon-Jon, the security guard outside the locker room. He was sixty, hypervigilant, with a mane of white hair. He rarely smiled, but grinned when he saw Lionel.

"You can't fix that?" he asked, nodding to Lionel's shoes as he scanned his frayed lanyard.

Lionel shrugged.

"Get some New Balance," Jon-Jon said.

"Thank you, no thank you," Lionel said.

"Maybe you get faster."

"I don't need to get faster."

"Hannah beat you again."

"Beat me how?" Lionel said, but didn't wait for the answer. He walked into the locker room and saw her, interviewing Hector Jimenez.

Hannah Tanaka was technically his competition, given they were the only two reporters who still covered the games for daily newspapers. Originally from Honolulu, Hannah wrote for the *Chronicle*, the larger of the two locals, both of which were treading water. But from the beginning she'd done everything humanly possible to help Lionel. When he'd started on the Giants beat, she introduced him to everyone in the stadium, shared every tip and data point, and he'd quickly fallen in love with her. She was so steady, so funny, her laugh raspy, almost lewd.

Squeak, squeak, squeak.

She had her notebook out, her phone—she had some transcription app that converted everything a player said to text, instantly—but when she heard him enter the room, she turned to Lionel and smirked. That smirk! Good lord.

She was married, though, had been married the whole time he'd known her, and had two teenage girls, and so every year Lionel had gotten better at disguising his heartache. During the games, they sat next to each other, bantering, complaining, comparing notes, and with every word she said, in her low, clenched-jaw way, he was stung by the great injustice of finding his favorite person, sitting next to her all day, but going home each night by himself, returning to his dark triangle, where he slept alone, in a building devoid of people.

"Hey Squeaky," she said.

"Hey Sis," he said. Calling her Sis, which he'd begun to do one day after she'd once called him Bro, kept him sane. *This is the line*, "Sis" said. *This is the line*.

Lionel looked around the locker room. There were only seven or eight players here this early, 10 a.m. on a day when the game would start just before one. The game didn't matter, so this didn't matter. There was no story on a team that was irrelevant. He could talk to the second baseman, Hollis, who had some kind of problem with his heel, but what was the point? Warren wouldn't give him space for news of another almost-injury to a player on a losing team.

Lionel saw Marco DaSilva. Marco had a hawkish face and a soft-serve body. He wore a backpack, two-strapped, and though he was only twenty-six, for some reason he did AM radio, where the average listener was seventy-six. "You hear about Gutierrez's OBX?" he asked.

Marco embraced every new statistical measurement and relished every acronym. Lionel had no clue what OBX was, so had to bluff.

"It was about what I expected," he said.

Lionel had learned to say this, or a variation on this, every time Marco was fondling a new metric. It conveyed that Lionel knew all, saw all, had seen every statistical assessment coming, was unsurprised and unimpressed. He walked away from Marco with an air of academic distraction.

Hannah finished with Jimenez and sidled theatrically up to Lionel. She smelled of sunscreen. She burned easily, she said. One of the reasons she'd left Hawaii.

"Behold the new guy," she said, and nodded to a gangly man in the corner. She handed him the day's media packet and pointed to the relevant section. "The PR department writes more than we do," she said.

This was true. Every game's media guide was four pages long, full of witty asides and inside jokes. It was longer, and felt far more alive, than anything Lionel was allowed to do. On the packet's second page, he found a short paragraph about a new middle reliever, Nathan Couture, being called up from AAA Sacramento. "Rivercat Grows Up, Becomes Giant," it read.

"Got here an hour ago," Hannah said. "Interview him before Marion puts the muzzle on."

The angular man in the corner was shirtless, holding the sleeves of his uniform apart, apparently dumbfounded to find his own name, COUTURE, stitched on the back of a Giants jersey.

Interviewing a rookie on his first day—Lionel had done it dozens of times, Hannah had done it hundreds of times. Still, Lionel had nothing better to do, and he'd never caught a player in the act of astonishment.

"Nathan?" he asked.

Nathan turned around slowly, nodding as if he'd

known that Lionel had been watching him all along. He smiled. His teeth were small, and he was missing one, the left canine; it gave him a look of youthful incompletion. He had a narrow, pockmarked face and a weak chin. A wispy, rust-colored mustache overhung his stern, chapped lips. His hair was long and greasy, his eyes maybe green, maybe brown. Finally he put on his jersey.

"First time in the bigs?" Lionel asked.

"Indeed," Nathan said.

That first word—it wasn't heard so much in a locker room. Lionel wrote "Indeed" in his notebook, and then asked the most inane, and most common, query in sports.

"How does it feel?"

It hurt to utter the words.

But Nathan nodded and inhaled and exhaled expansively through his nostrils, as if this was the most interesting and unexpected question he'd ever heard. He looked to the ceiling, then looked back to Lionel. His level gaze was startling, too—it was so rare that a player looked directly at any reporter. If they noticed a particular writer at all, it was with a quick glance—

furtive, wary, and generally free of respect or interest.

"When I got the call, just yesterday, I was elated," Nathan said. Lionel wrote down "elated" and under-lined it. There was an accent in Nathan's speech, too. Rural. Southeastern maybe. Georgia?

"The drive down from Sacramento was a fever dream," he continued. "The scenery rushed by like meltwater. And then to get here, to this cathedral, to warm up, and to meet these men at the top of their craft"—he swept his arm around the room, at a dozen players in towels and jockstraps; one was jiggling his leg, as if to awaken it—"and to be welcomed by them without condition, and now to see my name on this shirt... I have to say, it's sublime."

Lionel wrote and underlined "sublime." He looked around to see if he was being pranked. But no one was listening, no one was near.

"I'm sorry. I didn't get your name," Nathan said, and extended his hand.

"Lionel Gregorian," Lionel said, and shook it.

"Gregorian? Any relation to Vartan?"

Vartan Gregorian had been the president of Yale, then the commissioner of Major League Baseball, but that had been decades ago. He was long dead, and no one under thirty remembered him.

"No relation," Lionel said, and wrote down "heard of Vartan."

All this time, Nathan's gaze had not wavered. His eyes were very small but had the mysterious storm-swirls of gaseous planets. Now they rested on Lionel's notebook.

"Do you take shorthand?" he asked.

Lionel's handwriting was a chaotic mix of cursive and all caps—a madman's style. "No, no," he said. "This is just my personal code, I guess."

It was the first time in four years that any player had asked even the vaguest question about Lionel's process or profession.

"I assume you'll call me a journeyman," Nathan said. Lionel had just written that exact word. He quickly crossed it out.

"Don't, don't," Nathan said. "I like the word, and for me it's apt. And removed from baseball, it's a good word, don't you think? Journey-man. I know not everyone loves it, given it implies a kind of purgatory just below success, but in isolation, the word has a

13

simple beauty to it, right? How could you not want to be called a journey-man?"

Lionel looked at the word he'd obliterated on the page. "I guess so." He circled it. When he glanced up again, Nathan was looking down at him with priestly interest.

"Did you dream of this work as a boy?" he asked.

Lionel couldn't speak. He returned to the assumption that this was a prank. He had the impulse to flee. He looked around. No one looked back.

"I'm sorry. I shouldn't probe like that," Nathan said, and laid a hand on Lionel's shoulder. "I just had the sudden awareness that the two of us are in the enviable, even surreal position of living out our most impossible dreams. The fact that we aren't digging ditches or mining coal—that I'm paid to play a game and you're paid to watch a game and tell people what you see—it seems, in a world of sadness and misfortune, to be a thing of great luck. Don't you think?"

Lionel watched the game in a daze. He sat in the press box, Hannah to his right and Marco to his left, and read, and re-read, his notes, while hoping Nathan

Couture would be called in to pitch.

"Interesting guy?" Hannah asked.

"His numbers are shit," Marco said.

It was not right to withhold information from them, but Lionel kept the strange interview to himself. The Giants lost badly and Nathan didn't play, and somewhere along the way, Hannah, bored by Lionel's distracted state, moved to sit next to Marco, and made a show of having an especially good time with this new seating arrangement.

Lionel wrote up the story of the game, but because Nathan hadn't been a factor, it made no sense to include him. He'd play sooner or later, Lionel figured— at which point he could get him into a story. Maybe he could pitch a profile. Warren didn't generally like human-interest stories, and there was less and less room in the paper every day for them anyway, but maybe, for Nathan, he'd make an exception.

The next day, though, Nathan was gone, back to Sacramento. Which was not unusual. Players, especially middle relievers, bounced between the majors and minors with regularity. Sometimes they disappeared entirely.

Back in his apartment, the T-shirt shop, which was directly below, seemed to be working late; the sweet petrochemical smell of their ink and glue filled Lionel's room. Out the window, a sturgeon moon was rising to inconsequence while he looked up Nathan Couture. There was almost nothing about him. His hometown was Thomasville, Alabama. He was twenty-eight and had never been to college. His statistics were unremarkable in every way, so it was highly unlikely, Lionel realized, that he'd return to the majors, and certainly not for any stretch of time. He was both average and old.

Lionel gave up on writing anything about him. A mediocre pitcher who was happy to be in the bigs, and who asked about Lionel's work and method? What was he thinking? He went to the ballpark the next day and the day after, and wrote up his summaries of the games, and printed the players' inanities, and Marion baked him brownies, which were exceptional.

"I don't like her baking, actually," Marco said. He and Hannah and Lionel were watching batting practice on another cool August afternoon. It was five o'clock, with the game scheduled to begin at seven. A handful of kids, and a middle-aged man in an orange jumpsuit, were hanging near the dugout, waiting for autographs.

"Her cookies are brittle," Hannah said. Lionel hadn't thought about Marion's cookies that way before, but couldn't argue the point. They were definitely on the crumbly side. Soon all three of them had turned on Marion's baking, and all the food in the stadium, too.

"Much room for improvement," Marco said.

"I'm tempted to pack a lunchbox," Hannah said, and they all laughed. The food was free for members of the media, but it had gone downhill in recent months. The garlic fries, which had been so crisp last season, were now often less crisp, and the little pepperonis on the pizzas were less cooked than they had been before.

"Remember when they were sort of curly?" Lionel asked, and they all agreed that the pepperonis were better when they were cooked such that they curled. With the gates of complaint open, they aired their many grievances about life in the park. The architects of the park had not allotted enough elevators, so the writers often had to wait to get from the field to the press box. And the weather had been so-so, and given the uninspired start, the team was unlikely to make the playoffs, and the manager was not as communicative as he'd been the year before, and the crowds seemed less enthused, too.

"And the paper towels!" Marco wailed tragically.

In the bathrooms closest to the press box, the paper towel dispensers had been replaced by air dryers, which Marco and Hannah and Lionel all agreed were too loud for the task at hand. They all preferred paper towels. For a moment their minds all drifted to the halcyon days of the paper towel dispenser.

"Well," Marco said, his voice weary, "I guess we should get the lineup for tonight."

Back in the press box, Marion had placed the day's lineup, printed on crisp white cardstock, on each of their desks. Lionel examined his copy. After the batting order and starting pitcher, Lionel saw Nathan's name. He'd been called up again. Lionel felt a flutter of excitement that embarrassed him.

"Couture is back," Hannah said, and Lionel nodded, giving away nothing.

The game began, and Lionel did his usual thing,

typing out paragraphs about each inning that he could arrange later. The game seemed well in hand, the Giants up 5–0 in the sixth. It was highly unlikely they would need Nathan. He was the third or fourth middle reliever, and the starter was cruising.

But the Padres placed a series of hack singles in shallow left and right, and suddenly it was 5–3, then 5–4. The manager made his way to the pitcher's mound, took the ball, and the starter walked to the dugout, head low and muttering. Lionel looked to the bullpen wall to see who would emerge.

"Down in front!"

Lionel hadn't realized he was standing. Next to him, Hannah was giving him a quizzical look. Lionel sat down and stared at the far fence.

A narrow face emerged. It was Nathan. He stepped out of the bullpen, and for a moment he waited on the warning track, taking a long breath. The pause was not long enough to be noticed by anyone else, but Lionel knew Nathan was taking it in. This was the first time he'd be pitching in a major-league game.

He stepped onto the grass like it was the first step

of a royal staircase, and then broke into a steady trot. The rest of his entrance was unremarkable. He made it to the mound just as any other pitcher would, and started the usual preparations. He kicked the dirt and took his warm-up pitches. His face appeared on the massive outfield screen, in a goofy photo that emphasized his backwoods look, and twenty thousand fans wondered, idly, who he was. Then, without fuss, he struck out the first batter with three pitches.

"Damn," Marco said, and typed feverishly for a while. Lionel assumed he was looking for some numerical justification for what had just happened.

The next batter hit a rope over third. Winebrenner, the third baseman, knocked it down but bobbled it, and there was a runner on first.

"Let's see…," Marco said, and Lionel was sure he was looking for some model that tracked how Couture did with one out and a man on first. Couture threw a series of changeups and curves to the next batter, who finally hit a dribbler to second. Hollis ran it down, flipped it to the shortstop, who tagged second and hit the first baseman for a double play.

"Okay," Hannah said, "okay."

For Hannah, this was high praise.

Next inning, Nathan took care of the first three batters in much the same way—not with overwhelming power, but with crafty pitch selection and pinpoint placement. He struck out one, another grounded out, and the third fouled a ball high, and Nathan chased after it, briefly confusing the first baseman, who waved him off and caught it.

Between innings, Marco announced he was braving the commissary's dessert aisle, which, he'd heard, was offering a dairy-free sundae. Lionel was happy to be rid of him for half an inning.

"So...," Lionel began, but Hannah was on her phone.

"Huh," she said. Apparently Hollis, the second baseman, was getting an MRI. The heel that had been bothering him for weeks was now shot. Something had happened during that double play.

The closer pitched the ninth, as he always did, and that was that. The Giants won 5–4. Lionel took the elevator down to the locker room, where the mood was tense. The early word on the heel was bad. Hollis would be out for a while.

Lionel looked across the room and caught Nathan's eye. Warren would not want the story of Nathan Couture, not on the night the starting second baseman got injured. But Lionel wandered over to Nathan anyway. Most of the players had showered already and were changing into their street clothes. But Nathan was still in his uniform. It was spotless.

"Congratulations," Lionel said. "I see you still have your uniform on."

"Yeah," Nathan said. "Is that corny? I wanted to savor it for a bit longer." He pointed at his feet. "I changed my shoes, though." He'd swapped his cleats for sneakers.

Hollis walked into the room on crutches, and the reporters swarmed. The professional thing to do was to join them, and find out what was happening with the team's second baseman, who that year was being paid $12 million and was key to any playoff hopes. But Lionel stayed with Nathan.

"I noticed you paused when you first stepped out," he said.

"I did," Nathan said. "I assume you want to know how it felt?"

Lionel licked the tip of his pen theatrically.

"It was big," Nathan said.

Lionel wrote down "It was big," and for a moment wondered if Nathan's earlier eloquence had been a fluke. But Nathan's eyes were twinkling.

"Kidding, Lionel. Just kidding. Truly, I think it's a happy, wholly irrational spectacle," Nathan said. "Don't you think? I mean—"

"Hold on," Lionel said, and scrambled for his tape recorder. He couldn't get all this right with shorthand.

Nathan took a deep breath. "I mean, those upper-deck seats are probably two hundred feet up. Think of it. Twenty-five thousand people were here tonight, some of them sitting two hundred feet in the air, to watch men play as silly a game as has ever been conjured. Balls and bats and bases—all of it perfected and professionalized, sure, but essentially childish and irrelevant. And to serve it, to celebrate it, this billion-dollar coliseum is built. People come a hundred miles to watch it under a thousand lights. When you and I first met, it was a day game, a completely different atmosphere. At night the stadium takes on the look of

23

deep space. The sky is so black, the lights so white, illuminating a surreal sea of green. When you jog out there, as I did, in the dark, it feels, briefly, like you're in a spaceship, approaching a new planet."

Hector Jimenez, the catcher whose locker was next to Nathan's, had begun listening, and was giving Nathan a bewildered look. Lionel tried to bring Nathan back to Earth.

"There was some confusion over that foul ball," Lionel said, and already Nathan was nodding.

"First of all," he said, "that ball was rightfully Gutierrez's, and I should have known that. But it started out over my head, and the east wind took it toward the first-base line. So I had it in my sights. It was just a white dot in a black void. Then it rose higher, and the wind took it, and either *it* moved, or *I* moved, and suddenly it was gone. It dissolved, evaporated, transmuted! I mean, it ceased to be!"

Lionel wrote down "ceased to be" and caught Hector's eye. He looked horrified.

"And for a long moment," Nathan continued, "as I searched the void for the ball, I thought, What is this? How is this possible? I've caught a million balls.

How could I lose this one? And then I thought, Why
am I here? Where are my legs? Why can't I see? For a
second I really thought I'd entirely left this plane of
existence. The sky was so black, and this concrete
thing, this ball, had utterly disappeared in it! So I
wondered if it had been real, and if *I* was real, if anything was real."

Hector zipped his duffel bag and made for the
door.

"Then I smelled roast beef!" Nathan said, and
laughed loudly, and placed his hand on Lionel's shoulder. "I thought, Is that roast beef I smell? Who
brought roast beef to the ballpark? Then Cross yelled,
'Move, kid, I got it!' and my eyes swung toward him.
As they did, I saw the blur of a thousand stunned faces
in the stands. Then he caught the ball."

Marion appeared. She always grew suspicious
when interviews ran long.

"Everything good over here?" she asked. And with
that, the interview was over.

Lionel had to wait a few days, until the drama of Hollis's injury played out, to ask Warren for some space in

the paper for a profile of Nathan Couture. Warren had no interest in it at all, especially given Nathan hadn't played again since that first night. But then one day an ad dropped out, and Nathan was in.

So on page 31, below a piece about a local high school bobsled phenom, Lionel was given six column inches to introduce "Nathan Couture, Pitching Raconteur." Lionel suggested that headline, and no one cared enough to change it. Lionel had done little more than print the two long quotes he'd gotten from Nathan before Marion had hustled him away, but the article made an impression.

"You have to play me that tape," Hannah said. She didn't not believe the quotes were real. Lionel assured her they were.

All the reporters wanted to talk to Nathan, but Nathan was suddenly unavailable. Marion, risk-averse as always, felt they'd dodged a bullet by having this eccentric Alabamian talk and talk and somehow avoid a catastrophic mistake. She would not risk it again.

But then she changed her mind.

"The owner insisted on it," Warren said.

The octogenarian owner of the team had evidently

read Lionel's piece—he read only on newsprint—and was an immediate fan of Nathan's. He wanted more. He wanted Nathan in games, and wanted Nathan to talk, as much as he could, before and after games. It was generally assumed the owner was himself an eccentric (though from Kansas), and not long for this world. In any case, three days after Nathan's first game, he pitched the eighth inning of another tight game, and again he held his own, and the Giants won. This time, in a weird quirk of the batting order, he had to bat, and actually stroked a line drive into Triples Alley. Against the wishes of the first-base coach, Nathan rounded first base and was easily tagged out at second. It made for a very comical and eventful inning, and the home crowd went berserk.

Afterward, a scrum of reporters surrounded him, and Lionel, who had unwisely waited for the elevator, found himself in the third ring. Lionel felt proprietary, even jilted, and tried, in a way that filled him with shame, to get some kind of acknowledgment from Nathan that he was different, was special, that he had been first.

Nathan looked around at the throng before him,

and smiled broadly. "Well, this is extraordinary."

Hannah was closest, and asked the first question.

"General thoughts, Mr. Couture?"

There was some groaning and shifting among the reporters, because there seemed to be an unspoken understanding that their questions should be better tonight, for Nathan, this ungainly savant.

But just as he had with Lionel, he treated her banal question with the utmost seriousness. He looked at the ceiling for a long while, as if peeling the many layers of the query, then rested his eyes upon Hannah.

"First I thought about the smell of the grass," he said. "They cut it today, so the smell was fresh and just a bit sour, as newly cut is. There's something both crisp and funky there, something dead and alive, something wet and dry at the same time. I inhaled a bit longer than usual, wanting to take it in, and when I did, I saw four men, all in their seventies, arm in arm, in the stands, posing for a picture. Then the jumbotron showed a picture of the same men, as teenagers, at a ballgame. Same four guys, same pose, only fifty-odd years ago.

"And I thought about friendship—how crucial a

friendship like that is. Those men had been friends for
half a century, and I had the feeling that those men,
whenever they stand side by side, probably feel invin-
cible. And why they peg that friendship to baseball is
anyone's guess. Maybe it's the innocence of it. The
game, you know, hurts no one."

"Nathan, I—"

Another reporter, a national writer Lionel recog-
nized, broke in, thinking Nathan was finished. But
Lionel knew he wasn't. Nathan raised a finger.

"Then I saw a seagull. Maybe you did, too? It hov-
ered over home plate for a moment, maybe twenty feet
up. Under the lights it gave off an otherworldly glow.
It looked like a tiny angel. I wondered what brought
this bird, alone, to the ballpark. I assume he thought
he might come across some discarded chips or fries,
but the risk is considerable, too. Wouldn't the lights,
and twenty-five thousand people, be daunting? But
then again, he can fly. Is anything daunting when you
can fly? And briefly I thought about the nature of
flight. I do think there will come a time when humans
can fly more or less as birds do, and I wondered how
that would affect our idea of freedom. Will anyone

ever feel constrained, spiritually or materially, if they can fly?"

Lionel wrote down "if we can fly."

"And then it was time to pitch," Nathan said. There was scattered laughter, and the exchange of a dozen baffled looks. Nathan was stranger in person, they seemed to think, than he had been in Lionel's article. A dozen hands went up to ask the second question.

"Oh jeez," Nathan said. "I just went on and on. And you probably have so many other players to talk to. Why don't we do a speed round? Deal?"

The scrum reluctantly agreed.

Someone in front asked, "What was it like to get your first hit?" This was deemed a good question. The reporters went quiet.

"If you remember," Nathan said, "I fouled off the first two pitches. And fouling a ball off is like every mistake you make in life: you put everything you've got into a task, and if it's just a little wrong, it's wrong enough to make the whole effort a waste of time. The ball goes nowhere, or worse than nowhere. It's like a marriage annulled—so close to everlasting love, but in the end, a misuse of passion and trust."

The scrum thought he was finished, but Lionel knew he was not finished. His eyes brightened as he continued.

"But when you connect—when the barrel of the wooden bat hits the ball just so—you feel nothing. There's no resistance. Nothing at all. The ball leaps into the sky. The struggle is gone."

Marco edged in. "The spin rate on your four-seamer is 88, putting you ninth among middle relievers, but the exit velocity of the batters that hit you is 99.2, which is twenty-ninth. Do you have a plan to address that?"

As Marco was talking, Nathan's mouth gradually dropped open while his eyes narrowed. He looked like he was watching a kind of disgusting party trick. When Marco was finished, Nathan sighed.

"Honestly, Marco, I have no idea," he said.

A balding man in a baby-blue sweatsuit raised his hand. It was Tom Verlo, from the *LA Times*. He'd likely come upstate to throw a bit of cold water on San Francisco's new attraction.

"Can you tell us about running?" he asked. "You looked a bit rusty."

"Was it as bad as I'm thinking it was?" Nathan said, and flashed an enormous and spectacularly awkward smile, made more comic by his missing canine. "You know, as natural as it was when I hit that ball, running was the opposite. I felt like I was running in thousand-year-old armor. By the time I got to second, the ball was in the second baseman's glove. He was waiting for me like a groom would a bride. When he tagged me out, I was so relieved I wanted to fall into his arms."

Tom smiled. "On the broadcast, it looked like he said something to you."

"He did. He said, 'Mijo, now you can rest.'" Nathan looked at the clock on the wall. "We should hurry. Super-speed round now."

A young radio reporter raised her hand. "What does it sound like when a ball is caught?"

Nathan smiled.

"When I was a kid in Alabama," he said, "my grandfather lived in the backyard, in a little cottage. Every night after dinner, I would walk back to his place with him, and he would kiss me on the crown of my head, and say 'Adieu.' Then he would close the door, and the sound of his door closing would be a muffled, wet, and decisive click. That's what it sounds like when a ball is caught. Like the click of the door to my grandfather's home."

Nathan looked at the clock. "Thirty seconds left."

Now the questions came from all over.

"When you pitch, how do you get the ball to go where you want it to go?"

A moment passed when the reporters groaned.

"You know, I'm glad you asked that, because I have no idea," Nathan said. "I was taught each pitch, make no mistake about that. My dad and coaches taught me curves, splitters, changeups. Each requires a different grip, different release. But after that, how does the ball actually *do* what it does? On a changeup, why does the ball drop so late in the pitch? And why is the movement limited to that certain range? My own changeup only falls maybe five or six inches. Why not twenty? Why not two feet? Why does it do all it does at the exact moment when the batter most needs it to stay straight?"

No one knew.

"Okay, one last one? I see you, Lionel."

Lionel was standing in the back, taking it all in. He was happy for Nathan, and for the moment felt unnecessary. He shook his head.

"Nothing?" Nathan asked.

In that moment, there was something about the dynamic between them, the distance, too, that gave him an idea.

"Do you ever fear them hitting the ball back at you?" he asked.

"Yes. Yes, I certainly do," Nathan said, grinning his gap-toothed smile. "I have a rational mind, so most pitches, it's the *only* thing I think about."

That was the game, and the interview, that finally broke Nathan Couture into the national media. The next day, and for the following week, he was everywhere. ESPN did a segment, and Jimmy Kimmel had him on his show, where Nathan described the game as *entrancing*, *exacting*, *balletic*, and *inane*—four words no one had ever heard a player utter. With Nathan everywhere, and Marion offering him freely to all, the only thing Lionel could do was go to Phoenix.

Nathan's parents, though they'd raised him in Alabama, had moved to Arizona, and Warren green-lit a longer profile. In a stolen moment before a game, Lionel told Nathan he was thinking of going, and Nathan gave his blessing. "I trust you," he said.

"Thank you," Lionel said.

"You report accurately and you listen carefully."

"I try," Lionel said.

"They are tremendous people," Nathan said. "Immeasurably charming. You'll love them, and they you. I'm envious that you get to see them. I'll call ahead and let them know I vouch for you."

Lionel arrived at a comfortable ranch house twenty minutes from downtown Phoenix. In front, there was a pickup truck, and next to it, a small fishing boat rested on a trailer. The garage was open, and inside there was a tasteful Ford sedan and a new riding lawn mower. The walls were lined with neatly packed storage bins.

Lionel rang the bell. A descending series of electronic notes rang from within. When the door opened, a thin couple in their late sixties stood before him, shoulder to shoulder, arms around each other's waists. Jim and Dot, short for Dorothy.

"Lionel," Jim said.

"I took the liberty of pouring you a glass of ice water," Dot said.

Lionel followed them in. The house was dark, as houses used to be, with tiled floors. He walked on the side of his left foot, but the squeaking was clearly audible. Lionel guessed, correctly, that they would be too polite to mention it.

"Come sit," Jim said, and indicated a plush leather recliner in the living room. It was almost surely Jim's TV chair, and Lionel accepted the honor given. Nathan's parents sat to his right, on a matching couch.

"Nathan speaks highly of you," Dot said.

"He does," Jim agreed.

Lionel got his notebook out and looked around the room. He'd expected a house full of books, but there were few. There were no trophies, either—no shrine to their son, the professional baseball player. An enormous TV dominated one wall. Next to it were two school photos, both taken in middle school. One was clearly Nathan. The other was a girl, younger by a year or two, who shared a version of Nathan's goofy smile. But there was something knowing, even sardonic, in her eyes; she was the cleverer younger sibling.

"So how does it feel," Lionel asked, "with Nathan becoming this overnight sensation? The city's really taken with him."

"Oh, it's been so nice," Dot said.

"He worked hard," Jim said. "Deserves it."

Lionel smiled, thinking they were warming up. But they were done. They sat before him, wholly content to say nothing. Dot held her glass of water with two hands and smiled at Lionel in a motherly way. Lionel looked down at his notebook.

"So outside his skill as a pitcher," he said, "one of the things that's gotten Nathan noticed is his way with words. Was he always loquacious?"

Dot winced. She looked to Jim. Jim chewed his cheek.

"I read your first article," Dot said. "When you had him saying 'Indeed,' right away I thought, That's the comebacker." She pointed to her temple.

"He was never, you know, book smart," Jim added. "That was his sister."

"Never read a book unless you tied him down," Dot noted.

"He didn't talk a whole lot," Jim said, "and when he did, he did it in a regular way."

"He was all business. That's how his coaches described him."

"Single-minded."

"Then the comebacker happened," Dot said.

"I'm sorry. The comebacker?" Lionel asked.

"Well, he was hit by a comebacker," Jim said, sounding surprised that Lionel didn't know. "In Sacramento. It was on the radio up there."

"We were at the game," Dot said. "It was awful. Nathan threw a fastball to a very big guy, and this guy hit the ball right back at him a million miles an hour. Hit him right here." Again she pointed to her temple.

"From our angle it *looked* awful," Jim amended. "But later we saw it on tape, and it was more of a... It sorta grazed his head. The doctor checked him out and said he was okay. Nathan said he felt fine, so he pitched the rest of the inning. But then he took us out for dinner afterward, and it was like talking to some other person."

"He was really excited," Dot said.

"He had a ten-dollar word for everything," Jim

said. "He said the wine was 'unafraid.' That was new."

"He did say that. He said a lot of things," Dot said.

"He talked a lot that night," Jim added. "We flew home the next morning, and a few days later, he gets called up to the Giants. Which is when you met him."

"We figured the new way of talking was some temporary thing," Dot said. "But then your article comes out, and he's still talking this way—'indeed' this and 'glorious' that."

"His sister talked like that. She was the reader."

Lionel didn't want to ask.

"She passed young," Dot said. Jim held her shoulder close to his, as if to steady her, but she was sitting ramrod straight. "It was a tumor. When they found it, it was too big. I don't know why there had to be a tumor in my girl. It made no worldly sense."

Jim cleared his throat. "But with Nathan, when he was talking like that, we put it together. It had to be the comebacker."

Dot was nodding steadily, her eyes locked on Lionel. "Like something got knocked loose, and whatever was clogged up in there came pouring out. Sometimes people get hit in the head and start speaking another language."

Jim nodded enthusiastically. "French, Portuguese, sometimes Turkish. But seems like it's usually French."

By the time Lionel left, the sun was setting, and the impossible heat of paved Arizona had relented. He drove with the windows open, the red sunset behind him. He got back to the hotel and checked his messages. There was one from Hannah.

"Sorry about your boy," she said. "You probably know more than I do. Call if you want to swap notes."

Lionel looked online and quickly found a short blip about it. Nathan had been pitching in Cleveland when he blew out his arm. He left the park in a sling. The early word said it was a ligament. It was bad.

The professional thing for Lionel to do would be to return to Nathan's parents' home and get their reaction. But he couldn't bring himself to bother them, and was so shattered himself that he sat on the bed and stared at the wall for the better part of an hour. Finally he got to his feet, got to his rental car, and drove to the airport.

Word was that Nathan was coming back to San Francisco, to be assessed by the team doctor and by experts in the city. Lionel flew home and waited for news. For two days Nathan wasn't at the park, and no one had updates. Finally a press conference was called.

The room was full. Lionel sat at the back. The team doctor came out and explained the injury. They'd done an MRI and consulted with the best doctors in the city. Nathan would need surgery, and even after that, the prognosis was not good.

"I can't promise anything," the doctor said.

Lionel felt a presence at the back of the room. Marion had appeared behind him, standing against the wall. Finally Nathan walked in, wearing a coat and tie, his arm in a sling.

"I'm guessing you'd like to know how it feels," he said, and looked warmly out at the throng of reporters. But before he could begin, a man walked in late. It was the guy from the *LA Times*.

"What's the prognosis?" he asked.

The room groaned, but as always, Nathan treated the question with great decorum.

"If I were still eighteen," he said, "I might be able

41

to get the surgery. Then, in ten or twelve months, I could come back with reduced capacity. But I'm almost thirty. There is no way back. Even if I did every last thing right, I'd be, at best, a single-A player. And an old one at that."

Hannah was in the front row. She raised her hand.

"Hi Hannah," Nathan said. "I'm guessing you'd like to know how it feels?"

She laughed and lowered her hand.

"It's a good question. At the moment I'm still stunned. Numb. I have to admit my imagination had gotten ahead of me, and I saw great glory ahead. I was looking forward to the rest of the season, to seasons to come, to the lights, the faces in the crowd, all those people sitting two hundred feet in the sky to watch this game. It's over sooner than I'd expected, for sure. So for the moment I'm adrift. It was a gorgeous dream, and I wasn't ready to wake up. Don't you cry now, Hannah." He looked around the table for tissues. "All we have up here is water. Here," he said, and poured her a tall glass from a pitcher. And as he did, time slowed, stopped. Every reporter in the room watched closely, as if they'd never before seen water move from one vessel to another.

Finally Nathan sat down again, and called on Lionel. "Did you have any warning?" Lionel asked.

"You know, my friend, I really didn't. I felt good that day in Cleveland. But it's probably like any other thing. How can a sequoia withstand a thousand years of earthquakes and fires and wind, and finally, one day it just falls? One afternoon, a gust comes and it gives up." Nathan stood. "I'll miss you all. Hope I see you here or there or somewhere in between. Goodbye now."

Lionel walked onto King Street, trying to figure out how to shape the story, or if he should bother at all. He hadn't written about his time with Nathan's parents yet; his heart wasn't in it. And as juvenile as it was, he was deflated that Nathan hadn't reached out to him since the injury. It was silly to think they had a different kind of bond, given all he'd had was a one-day head start, but still.

He knew he should be among people, but he walked toward his apartment, planning to spend the night alone. When he turned the corner at Second Street, though, he felt a presence next to him.

"Caught up to you!" It was Nathan, out of breath. He was still in his coat, but had taken off his tie. It was in his hand, in a blue tangle. "I tried to find you at the park, and then was wandering around the neighborhood, hoping to run into you. I know you live around here. Then I heard the squeaking."

They ducked into a burrito place. Lionel tried to order margaritas for them both, but Nathan declined. "I don't know why my mind is working the way it does now, but I don't want to mess with it." He ordered a lemonade. "You go ahead, though."

Lionel ordered a lemonade, too, and they sat by the window facing the park. "Your parents told me about the comebacker," he said.

"Yeah, I figured," Nathan said. "Funny thing is, I don't feel different, and I don't see differently than I ever did before. I've always noticed the same things, but now I have the need, and maybe the words, to describe them."

"You'd make a good sportswriter," Lionel said.

"Oh, I don't know," Nathan said, and he paused, his eyes drifting. "My sister was the eloquent one. She could write, too. My parents mention her?"

"They did," Lionel said.

For a second Nathan smiled, as if thinking of her, of something she'd said. "Anyway," he said, "for now I'll leave the reporting to you. I'll be reading, making sure you get it right."

"I can do better," Lionel said suddenly, and Nathan did not argue the point. I really have to do better, Lionel thought. It was criminal to sit in that park, with all that color, all that vaulting joy in a world of sadness and misfortune, and not do better.

"You plan to fix the squeak?" Nathan asked.

"I took it back to the shoe guy," Lionel said, "but he freed himself of any responsibility."

"Can I?" Nathan asked, and Lionel took off his shoe and handed it to Nathan.

"It has to be an air pocket, right?" Nathan said. Even with one bum arm, he quickly found the pocket and aimed a fork at it. "Can I?" he asked again. Nathan gave his consent, and Nathan jabbed a strategic hole. "Try it now."

Lionel put the shoe back on and walked a few steps. The squeak was gone. His relief was immeasurable. "Thank you," he said.

They finished their lemonades and stepped back into the city. The lights were on in the stadium. Lionel had forgotten there was a home game that night. He turned to Nathan, thinking he'd be wistful, but his eyes were sharp and happy, like a father looking at an old photo of a grown son who'd turned out well.

"So what will you do now?" Lionel asked.

"I've been thinking about that. Are you walking this way?" Nathan was headed toward the water, his gait loose.

Lionel followed. "Maybe you buy out my shoemaker."

Nathan laughed. "You know," he said, "a few years ago, I was in a high rise in Guangzhou, visiting a friend at his office. Long story. But anyway, this was forty-two floors up, and there was a man outside, cleaning the windows. The man was on one of those platforms that goes up and down outside a building, and he had one of those wide T-shaped tools for cleaning the glass—you know the tool. So simple, like a blade. He drenched the window with soap, applying it with such liberality. Just *soaked* this vast window overlooking this limitless city."

46

Nathan turned to the bright towers of downtown San Francisco. "And then, with the blade, he slashed the surface of the glass with the precision and finality of a guillotine. He got every last white sud. As we watched, the view through the window went from muddy to crystalline."

Lionel couldn't figure out what the connection was. Nathan wanted to be a businessman in a Chinese high rise? And how did this minor-league pitcher from Alabama end up with a friend in Guangzhou?

"So I thought I'd like to do that job," Nathan said. He meant cleaning the windows. "Not necessarily in Guangzhou, and not forever, but I'd like to try that for a while. I like being outside."

They'd reached the water, and Lionel thought he should get back to the ballpark. His job was to write about the games, after all. He reached out to shake Nathan's hand, and Nathan lowered his sling, his eyes suddenly alight.

"Or babies!" he said. "You know how after babies are born in hospitals, there are nurses who hold the babies while the moms recover from the birth? How do you get that job?"

Lionel didn't know. Nathan released Lionel's hand and began backing away, toward the South Beach marina, where a hundred white masts pointed into the night like lances.

"Imagine holding babies all day!" Nathan said. "Wouldn't that be a worthwhile life? So tomorrow I'm going down to the maternity ward to find out who gets to hold the babies before they go home."

DAVE EGGERS is the author of *The Eyes & the Impossible*, *The Every*, and *Heroes of the Frontier*, among other books. He is based in the San Francisco Bay Area.

ACKNOWLEDGMENTS

The author would like to thank Susan Slusser, beat reporter for the San Francisco Giants, for her kindness, hospitality, expertise, encouragement, and sly wit. Also thanks to Andrew Baggarly, Brandon Crawford, and John Brebbia for answering bizarre questions with humor and rare intellectual elasticity.

This story was carefully, classically, and classily edited by Ann Hulbert, fiction editor of *The Atlantic*. Thank you also to Adrienne LaFrance, for first championing it.

Thank you for early reads and help along the way: Dave Pell, Amanda Uhle, Amy Sumerton, Eli Horowitz, and VV. Thank you also to Lindsay Williams, Brooke Ehrlich, Angel Chang, and Caitlin Van Dusen.

Author proceeds from this book go to McSweeney's
Literary Arts Fund, helping to ensure the survival
of nonprofit independent publishing.

www.mcsweeneys.net

McSweeney's, founded in 1998, amplifies original voices
and pursues the most ambitious literary projects.

WE PUBLISH:

McSweeney's Quarterly Concern, a journal of new writing

The Believer magazine, featuring essays, interviews, and columns

Illustoria, an art and storytelling magazine for young readers

McSweeneys.net, a daily humor website

An intrepid list of fiction, nonfiction, poetry, art and
uncategorizable books, including the Of the Diaspora
series—important works of twentieth-century
literature by Black American writers